AN AISLE OF BLOOD

IS THIS THE FUTURE?

SANIA AHMED

Sania Ahmed (Author)

Solely dedicating this book to all my friends and the people who love to indulge themselves into a world of depth and fiction. A place without chains and and no rules to exist. A place, where imagination takes flight, and we fly feeling the overwhelming pleasure within. Looking forward to your love and appreciation!...

- Sania Ahmed (Author)

Contents

Acknowledgements

Writing is a not a skill of words but the view of eyes..The way one percieves is the way one notes, the prettiest of all ...This book is not only my work, but the hardwork along with constant undying support of all my friends ...

I would specially like to thank **Mr. Shlok Bhardwaj** and **Md. Mehadi H. Siddique** for penning down the whole of my book, so that I concentrate on the story. Being beyond thankful to my friends **Ms. Violina Baruah, and Ms. Shraddha Singha,** for their unconditional motivation and the role they played, always staying beside me and being my support. Not to forget mentioning, expressing my heartfelt gratitude and thankfulness to **Maam Agnes Kamei (Little Flower School)** for evaluating my book and claiming it as worth a publish. "Very good, keep it up!" were the words, that felt like a pat on my back. There couldn't be a greater fuel than this for me to complete my book. Anticipating your love and support as you dive into this world of fiction that I created!

Preface

People think time is like a river that flows swift in one direction, but time has its own faces which sometimes owe us to break our limits and cut through the waves that stop us from flying.

There are many things that can inspire us to write. The rivers, the trees, or even our dreams. But uniquely, my credit of writing completely goes to games and just games. Through the games I've played, I've learned that there are no chains to imagination. Here's my favorite quote from someone belonging to the world of gaming-

"If you move on and you find enemies on your way, this means that you are on the right path"

- Anonymous

This quote speaks of the society. The people that judge behind, but there should be no turning back. According to my school of thoughts, we all have one life and it's on us how we choose to live it. We must be bold, fearless and live it to the fullest.

In this book, I have put my imagination forward to write upon the adventurous story of Vika along with her companions. A journey defying fate. A journey to save lives, to save the world. Will we need to fight for it, is this the future?

Sania Ahmed

Prologue

I opened my eyes and the world around me seemed blurry. I sat up on my bed and my body began feeling like a rusted machine that just laid in the corner since long. I took a deep breath and finally pulled up my lazy body and walked towards my window, suddenly I got stuck with a feeling that i had lost my past, all that i remembered was me myself and my dad 'Franklin'. Dad and I meant the world to each other,we were more like friends that was far better than living in a serious dad-daughter thing.

After thinking a lot of these stuff I filled a glass with water and removed the curtains of my window; just to see a view that made the glass slip out of my hands, my eyes widened as the glass broke intoa thousand shards....Everything outside seemed like an uninhabited ghost town, there were flies and bats instead of those beautiful butterflies and melodius birds that sang a song of spring...

All my eyes could see were laid down telephone towers and a ghostly neighbourhood. I suddenly got a feeling that an earthquake struck last night and i overcame it all with my great skill of sleeping!, but why was everything quiet instead of people trying to make things good? I ran down to look for dad, I could already hear him playing my favourite song on his rustic-vintage looking guitar. I called out to him as loud as I could, dad got up and hugged me tight and said "Vika, finally I see you speaking to me or it is another one of my dreamy hallucinations!?". Dad looked quite a lot different than I saw him yesterday, he had a long beard, but how could that happen in just a night?

I asked dad "What do you mean dad?" " Seems like youv'e got a great deal to know" he replied. I sat on the couch right infront of him and finally questioned to get an answer that changed everything. "What exactly happened dad, the world around appears very different ". I asked wanting a reply as fast as he could speak. Dad's face turned pale as he remarked "You were in a comma since the last 5 years, and as you can see things got a lot of change in them."

I really thought he was joking but the seriousness in his voice spellbounded me. How is this even possible, What exactly happened to me and was still happening in the world outside the door. I wanted an answer even though I knew I couldn't get it from myself . I asked this to dad, but he didn't reply, and his silence made me catch an eerie feeling. I rushed back upstairs got dressed with the clothes that were new to me, I really was in a comma I really had grown up a lot and if i calculated right I was 19 now...Thinking such things I stared at myself and then ran downstairs to go, meet up my friends. How much they would've missed me, I thought.

I moved towards the front door and to my surprise it was all chained and locked up, dad saw me trying to open the front door and he came running behind he held my hand hard and squealed "What exactly are you trying to do Vika!?"

-"Dad i need an answer to my questions and if you are not answering them I wanna know it from my friends" I said being rude."Who do you think will answer your questions? The zombie or the lifeless bodies that lay near and far?" Dad too replied being harsh. I kept mum for a momemt or two and then I spoke up again "Dad, what happened" I asked being quiet low. Then dad began narrating my life till that moment which seemed like a story..What was it?

1

My life

"You and me , we both meant the world to each other and still do. I fulfilled every wish of yours when you were a young lovely child , but that one dark night detached you from me and after that what not had happened. You and I went to your favorite place back then, 'the aquarium' ,the turtles, dolphins the happy children all around. But all that mattered to me was your smile, while we were returning back you started to cry out for an ice-cream, so I made you stand in the corner and walked past the street to the cart...I never knew that you would run behind me, a car..."

Thats all he could tell me, his eyes filled but he never cried infront of me nor did he ever fell weak.

"Lunch time, i guess? So miss what would you like to have" he spoke trying to cope up with the situation "Some 5 year old food or you fine with your salines huh?" he added "I dont even remember what were the names of the food" I replied frankly so that he could feel better. Dad bought me a mere lunch comprising of bread and garlic oil but I didn't question anything for i was actually using my teeth after a really long time I feel. After lunch I turned on the TV but there was no signal, only back and white dots buzzing around, and I dont know why I recklessly stared at them? I know that was unearthly but well, nevermind...

-"Dad maybe there is something wrong with this thing" I confusingly called up to him.

-"Its been like this since the past one year" he replied, just then the doorbell rang and to my surprise it was my childhood friend ***Jonathan****, dad said that he came regularly to visit us...that really made me respect him and his love for friendship much more than ever before. He looked at me and smiled and his smile spoke to me as if he was the happiest man on the planet at that moment, "Have grown up to be even more prettier miss Vika" he remarked as he held me tight in his arms. He was the one after dad whom I had met after 5 years. He sat down beside me and we talked about everything after*

a while i got the right moment to ask him about, why the things after 5 years instead of looking futuristic , looked descructive and lifeless. :"your'e so lucky you passed over the whole thing without even knowing a bit of it" he began..

*"**Dr. Xuan**, a famous scientist in the field of genetic science, he was working on his latest project, a vaccine that was meant to make humans capable of working day and night , which meant that the vaccine would complete the requirement of the person's sleep. Like all other vaccines this vaccine too was tested on an animal, 'a rat'. Doctor injected the vaccine on the rat and left it alone in a glass box and went away to get the results of his experiment the following day, the whole internet buzzling and waiting for the outcome, but to the fate of the world and its people the next morning the rittle rat went missing, the first case of this apocalypse was found on 17 february 2862. It was found that the first person infected was seen getting bitten by a rat or maybe 'the rat'."*

-"An apocalypse? What happened to the person who was bitten?" I showered him with questions as he paused for a while. Then he continued.."The person bitten, started behaving abnormally and became brain dead, after which it was spread by him biting his own family members , as they too began turning into those

walking dead"

-"walking-brain-dead? Do you mean zombies?" At the beginning everything seemed to be thrilling, but as the conversation deepened those things began to haunt me.

-"Soon the virus spread all over the world turning it into a global pandemic and now we humans are on the verge of extinction..when bitten by the infected, some die and the rest carry out as zombies biting people to add to thier population. They only die when shot on the forehead, I have got a lot of experience in that you know?" he stopped sipping into a glass of water.

-"Have you been into killing zombies for the whole one year and where are the other friends? I questioned him.

-"Well if your'e asking about our friends the one's alive are You, me, Joe and Liana and I dont know where they live now and not even sure if they are still alive but we saw everything happening right infront of our eyes" he sighed.

-"What happened to the rest of the friends ...? Did they too...?"

-"Yes" he stopped me and resumed "they too turned into zombies and had to be shot.."

-"You mean I will never get to see them ever again? Why did you kill them? Wasn't there a cure? " tears rolled down my eyes as i questioned my heart out..

-"Till now, this thing is going on, its been a year already , and no cure to be found, this place, few years ago was inhabited by fifty thousand people but now only 50-60 people are alive in my sight. Everyone goes out for one thing and that is food, it will be very soon that we are gonna starve. It's only this town to my vision where the people are alive, every other place had turned into a jungle and few buildings that stand creepily with zombies, they are a kind of their residence". I kept quite as a thousand things were running in my mind but I said nothing for a while.

-"Do you know the place where it all began?" I asked.

"Are you upto something, if yes let me tell you its not at all safe outside and every 5 minutes a zombie is found trying to attack the last of us, good thing this apocalypse made everyone know how to use guns" He said being protective.- "But if not us then who? We must go to that place, there must be a cure... I got stopped by a slam on the door. "You are not going anywhere Vika" dad exclaimed. I did not say anything but noticed him keep his gun and the bullets in the drawer near the front door. Jonathan knew everything that was going on, on my mind. He looked at me and said a 'No' shaking his head slightly. Dad asked Jonathan to stay with us that night and he agreed. At around 1:00 a.m. I woke up with a sound just below my window, I ran and unfolded my curtains just to see dad struggling to get away with a zombie, that thing; it had fungus grown on its face, I was so shocked I could not even call out to Jonathan for help. Dad...was bitten, I stood by the darkness of my heart as I lost the only reason of living. I immediately ran down picked up dad's gun and shot that zombie form my room window. I ran down to see dad, I saw him laying down..I went closer..his eyes started rolling up, I with the strongest of will I ever had I closed my eyes and used another bullet of the gun..on my dad. I then rightly knew how it feels to lose someone dear to you, at that instant I got a new reason to live ***To save the world...***

2

The Journey Begins..

I went near Jonathan and sat down beside him, lost in thoughts, as I spent the rest of the night sleepless. Early morning when he woke up, I told him everything that happened, he promised me that he'll be with me and protect me forever. I stood up and exclaimed-

"It's our time now and we need to save the rest of the people alive". "What do you mean Vika? Are we..." I did not let him complete the sentence. "We are going to the place where these things began, there must be a cure". "Vika, please it will be no less than jumping into well, maybe someone else who's stronger can do it" he spoke.

"Everyone thinks the some Jonathan, everyone just sits down to let someone else do it, but if we

too do the same I believe there will be no man walking on this planet ever again." The fire in my eyes filled him up with a feeling of self-esteem, which led him to be a part of the most unusual and adventurous journey of my life...

After two days of planning, mapping and collecting all the required supplies we began the journey that was 250 miles long, no vehicles to be found so it was, whole way walking and exploring the new, dark world. It felt like the last time I am seeing my birthplace, I turned back as my eyes signed a pleasure goodbye to the place, Jonathan could feel me, he put his hands around my shoulder and we, moved on...

3

Beauty Shatters to darkness

After walking about 2-3 miles we found a place where the time seemed to stop, the grass moved slowly as the midday sun shone bright, right above us. "Prepare your guns!" Jonathan raised his voice, "Are you sick, this place looks completely safe" I replied. But all he did was give me a sarcastic smile maybe to tell me how unknown I was, the situation was quite awkward but suddenly we saw around just to find five to six zombies walking towards us. He shot 4 of them and I managed to kill the rest. "Doesn't it feel like a shooting game?" He said as he laughed and watched me struggle to reload my gun.

"Do you know the second zombie I shot ever in my life was Dad" my voice turned low.

"Oh! Vika don't be sad it's you who taught me to face my problems and to be strong at any circumstances of my life" he said trying to calm me down. I looked directly into his eyes and that's when undoubtable trust was born between us, after resting for around 10 minutes, we carried on with the journey but to both of our surprise, after moving a little forward we came across a watch tower, we went closer to it and finally found another set of humans inhabiting that place but fewer than the ones on the society I lived. They were all military officers and they informed us that they stay up all night to kill those zombies and protect anyone who's alive. Just then we all heard a 'grrr' sound and I laughed cause it was Johnathan's hungry stomach, they were generous enough to offer us food even during this crisis, we did not tell them anything about our mission and that we were not even halfway to the destination.

-"If you pull things this long, we will surely be late for everything" I whispered into his ear angrily. He stood up, infact we both stood up "Thank You so much officers, that is really so heroic of you that you skip sleepless nights to protect people, and thank you so much for that food, my stomach really begged some" he spoke

as he was half drunk though he wasn't "Thank you officers wish you luck!" I said as I pulled him outside their cabin in order to continue what we were really doing. On the way we also collected supplies like grenades, bullets etc that lay near the dead bodies of I don't know human, zombies or maybe both.

Throughout that day we completed around 10-15 miles of the expedition after which the sun went down and bring about immense darkness, the place where we stopped was an abandoned village so, we had roof under which we could spend the whole night. We slept in the early evening so by maybe 3:00 AM we were back with all the energy to start a new day, but food was still a problem. Then I looked though my bag-pack in order to find something that maybe edible and voila! I found a packet of biscuits in my bag. I looked at Jonathan as maybe it was the last hope for us all through the journey also no one was sure that we'd find something to eat even at the destination, but that day the biscuits felt like the sweetest berry carried down from the heaven... hunger made me feel that!

1 day just flew by and it was a new day as we started again for our destination 'the D Tower' ,well that was the place where Dr. Xuan did he researches and also the birthplace of this virus...

4

A Lone secret

A few hours of walking suddenly the dark clouds folded above us and the rain showered heavily, we ran and took refuge under a tree, a very huge tree indeed! The tree leaves formed a kind of canopy and completely prevented the rain. One hour passed and it kept on raining and I being impatient enough, began strolling around the tree just then, I noticed a hole like that of rabbit's burrow and out of my immense curosity, I peeped into the hole and the things inside turned out to vary a lot from my expectations...

First of all, there was a ladder that led down to a way that was about 100m deep. "Jonathan, I know we are getting late but we definately gotta check this out" I screamed out of curosity and he hurriedly arrived near me to reveal himself the passage to an unknown secret. Well secrets are usually unknown if we keep them to us!! After getting down the ladder we came across a normal sized iron door which was definately locked from inside. I knocked but no one came to recieve us the door, then Jonathan started slamming the door and suddenly, the door opened with a voice familiar to my ears.

-"You guys survived staying outside, that's brave of you!" the girl said as she faced her back towards us.

-"Do I know you or maybe it's like we've met earlier" I queried. She turned back and to my surprise it was Liana another one of my dearest friend.-"Vika, you are the one I missed the most, Joe's with me too, Oh Joe! where are you, look we have someone special here" Liana was so happy and tears rolled as a sign of her immense joy to see the both of us. Joe came out running and hugged me tight and now we were a squad. The four of us sat down together in Joe and Liana's cozy underground base as I narrated the whole story beginning from dad's death to the mission that both me and Jonathan began and it turned out to be everyone's dream to accomplish, no other aim in life but to find the cure, no other hope but oneself.

Liana too lost her whole family and Joe did not even know if anyone of his blood was alive. Joe and Liana stayed together whole through this time and gradually fell weak for each other. And all through this apocalypse they built their own world in a underground base that was definitely a very safe shelter at this situation. I definitely knew, love was a nothing but a new form of weakness and I never wanted to be weak. I really hated love, but everytime I looked at Jonathan's eyes I felt it was not that bad...

I was lost in thoughts as the rest of the crew discussed, what we are to do...

5

A new start..

After spending about 4 days in the cozy base, we finally raised our heads to sunshine and there started a new journey...

We ventured deep through forests which were actually cities a few months ago. Broken street lights, deconstructed buildings and useless cars. So, as
soon as night fell, nothing except the moon and stars were visible therefore surviving a night was a real challenge.

2 nights passed as we moved 45 kilometers more and closer to our destination and by this two nights we have killed more than 100 zombies. For few days we had food and everything that was required but after a few days shortage of literally everything struck, no food, no drinking water therefore it always felt like everything was dry and deserted up. But actually it was not like that, it was the recent end of monsoon and there were pools of water inhabited by dead bodies. I remember the last day it rained was the day when we visited Joe and Liana.

"Rise and Shine guys" I exclaimed as I was the first one waking up sleeping in the middle of nowhere, in destroyed 'shopping mall' maybe. All of them woke up at once but their faces had that one irritated look similar to which we give when early
morning when the alarm clock rang it's life out, specially in cold winter mornings. How cozy were those when I happily held dad's hand we talked all the way to school.

I started daydreaming becoming the centre of everyone's weird look, when I came out of my dream world we all had great laugh together, that soothed many of those dark, deep thoughts in my mind.

Well, after all that we made a decision that we all should spend one more day in that building looking for supplies as we were now about to begin walking through the huge grassland that stretched for miles. Luckily enough we found

many things like
some bullets, some shot gun ammo, 2 grenades and a cool electric stun-gun. We also filled our bags with bandages and all such stuff from the mall's medical store, that too was definitely (as thought) destroyed but we managed to find out a lot of useful things.

At last night fell and the boys managed to light a fire, we all sat down together, all were silent and continuously staring at the fire. "Hey guys, don't make this so emotional, be cool fellas" Jonathan spoke.
"Bro, there's no energy left in me to speak, just one more day without food and I die..." Joe replied. "Shut up dude be calm", I said as my eyes fell on a lone tree quite around 500 meters away, "we may have some hope" Liana exclaimed as she read my eyes.
Joe and Liana stayed back and we both (Jonathan and me) headed towards the tree but as we neared it we started to realize it definitely was not a tree bearing fruits, but on moving further we noticed a dead man and a huge sack beside him, the man's body was half rotten and the bones stuck out. Ew! that scene was the most haunting part of all. Jonathan took his gun out, pointed it from 'right to left' and opened the sack.

"Looks like we've got our hopes up" he claimed as I peeped in the sack to see a whole lot of packaged food (like biscuits, drinks, chips, etc). "Looks like this man came out in search of food" I sighed. Jonathan nodded with a sad feeling but that food was enough to last for a week or two.

We had our food and filled our bags with the rest and we were now ready to continue the next morning.

6

Obstacles form the way

Next day all of us got up early and packed up our things and hopes, as we planned that we will not sleep until we cross the grasslands as it was really dangerous. We walked and walked and walked, almost all the places looked but we followed our track and by the end of the midnight we finally reached a ravine where we all got some time to rest, I gazed at the beautiful stars above, just wishing that our efforts do some good...atleast.

After a while, we all continued heading towards our destination, and now we were walking through abandoned cities/towns, trust me that was much more creepier than walking through those grasslands or forests, but now I was used to killing those zombies, everytime they emerged I smirked and 'head-shot'.

After completing another trek we reached to a place where a fair was held many months ago. Destroyed play areas, toys and wait... there was a circus tent, we heard some noise coming from there and immediately headed towards it craving for some survivors. We went inside the half-torn dusty tent and a sudden silence (a creepy one) began to spread. Suddenly my eyes fell on a zombie and I shot it but as soon as I did so, hundreds of them emerged out of nowhere (or maybe everywhere), we got coverged from all sides, no way out. We all got our guns out and, were shooting them mercilessly, suddenly one of them crept from under all our eyes and Liana, was captured. She got bitten on her ankle Joe went towards to save her but he too was about to be caught but just in time, the zombie was shot. After we killed (hopefully) all of them present there, Liana was the second one I saw practically turning pale, eyes rolling up and Joe hugging her tight but this time too I with my eyes filled-to-rim, had to kill her. "Joe keep yours hopes up, we have to save a lot others who are someone's own" Jonathan explained and Joe, he sat on the muddy floor and kept staring at her, his eyes flooded because his life was now lifeless now. Liana's death brought along the first obstacle that we had on our way.

-"You get rid of my eyes and save whomever you like, did she not mean anything to you?

How can you just, even think of moving on, Vika never expected this from you atleast". Joe thundered, as it was the first time I saw him this angry". Jonathan got hyped at this...

-"What do you think we should do? Sit here whole life and cry? What's gone is gone, nothing can happen now and if you keep up with this attitude of yours, I'll love it if you stop here to spend the rest of your life making 'great uselessness of time". "Yes, Joe we have to keep moving lest there will be someone who gets separated from their loved-ones everyday, every minute." I tried to make him calm down. Suddenly he got up picked his backpack and spoke as he faced his back towards us "Wish you luck, I will love not be a part of your journey, do it yourself, for yourself, I've lost hopes and even if I die I will not regret it."

-"But...Joe"

He walked away briskly as I tried to stop him, Jonathan grasped my hand and said "Let him be on his own, else someday, I fear he can do anything to out of his envy and fierceness". I looked into his eyes as we got separated again and we planned that we were enough to make the things work the way they did, that night my eyes could not rest the whole night and I kept thinking of Dad and Liana...

7

Wilderness Awaits..

Next day too we had the same schedule woke-up, biscuits for breakfast and start moving, this went on for 15-16 days and we kept moving, spending alternate sleepless nights, i.e. one day he slept, the other day I did, in this way we had our rest as well as both of us could sleep carelessly. One night, when we were a bit more than halfway to our mission, I and he sat down and that day too we had a fire lit up in-front of us.

-"Can I ask you something I hesitated " Yeah sure Vika, its only you and me who will you ask if not me" Jonathan replied. "You really care for me a lot, I see. You really mean a lot, thank you so much for everything that you do for me" I let my feelings speak. "Ayy you dumbo! whom should I care for if not you? You are the sweetest friend I have" he laughed, but I surely knew that

there was something else that was going on his mind, he really behaved weird sometimes.

"I think it's best that we look for a car" he tried his best to change the topic and I too didn't want to offend him. "We saw lot of cars on our way till here and the fact is, we need them working both physically and mechanically I guess". "That's so clever of you Miss Vika, I never knew we need them working" he taunted me "Youu!!" I exclaimed as we had a sort of cute-fight.

That was enough of us, wasting our precious time and conclusion was made that, the particular day's mission was to find a 'vehicle', finding a mean of transport would really boost up our mission and this book wouldn't be so long! We looked, found and tested many cars but always, our expectation (of them not working) came true.

We looked far and wide by this we traveled a few more kilometers pedestrially.

One day, as though everything was going fine but the fate looked on to a new adventure. We climbed up a hill and looked up to see a new, interesting problem...

8

Now what...?

My eyes captured a deep, very deep ravine and there were only two ways to cover over that ravine.

i. To use the only cable-car that hanged destroyed on the other side

ii. Fly over it... which was definitely not possible until life is at fiction. Therefore the first way seemed a bit more appropriate, the cables were strong and could definitely carry a good amount of weight but we needed a carrier using which we could cross that thing. I sat down tensed thinking at a way out of this, just then on idea sparked our minds together 'zip-line', all we had to do was somehow fix ourselves strongly with the cable and the leave it to luck. Though 'luck' was the worst thing on Earth, all that was left now was to believe it, eyes close and completely leave it to the cable, as our death could completely change the new world that we we live today.

We started searching for many of the required materials to build up the belt, that we could trust on, after spending almost more than half of the day all we found was some flat tires, electricity cables, iron rods and few pieces of rope but what could be made out of 'em? Well that was the question at that hour, after spending so much of energy on finding these useless stuff my brain haulted it's thinking capacity and I sat on the grass and I caught sight of one of the most most beautiful sunsets that could ever be, but sun setting down and darkness that came along was a sign that we lost for the day.

Few days, we spent trying to squeeze out our brains to find the best we could do, but always ended up with the same question... 'Now what?'.

9

A pleasant surprise.

We tried the best we could but nothing seemed to fit the way they should. Jonathan begruded, and I felt making a rocket was much easier than crossing this stupid trench, another day went by and the sun began lowering down suddenly we could hear a perplexed sound, I recognized the sound and it was "A Helicopter?" we exclaimed together, it seemed like it was looking for us, we shouted our heart out "Help, Help! We're down here".

And soon without much of our effort the helicopter landed right beside us but the surprise still awaited. The helicopter only had the pilot and the pilot was,

- "Joe". Jonathan was unexpectedly happy to see him. "Hey bro, never thought you'd show up

again"

-"Me neither, but the only people that were left in my life were you both and my heart couldn't betray you." Joe regretted him behaving rudely with us but that
was a completely normal behaviour at that consequence.

-"How'd you manage this helicopter?, and where were you these past weeks?" I queried.

-"Well they both have a same answer, the weeks I spent at a camp and gained their trust to borrow this metal body" he smirked. "We really required this one bro, but now I suggest that we fly over this before it gets darker". "Sure ma'am" I got a prompt reply from the boys, and there we flew above the trench which had a river flowing deep down and due to the sun setting the red sky made the river look like an 'Aisle of Blood' and if consequenced with the situation, it was definitely correct to feel so. Soon, we covered a lot of distance and it was a great boost, we kept flying the whole night and we conquered around 85 kilometers, but how could stuff be this easy right?

My worst expectation and the expected reality combined to burn up 90% of the fuel of the 'copter', we had to land urgently, as if we flew longer it would end up getting crashed so, we landed as soon as possible and it was the earliest part of the day, just before the sun showed up, the sky was pinkish-purple as the stars slowly began to fade away and bright sun- light conquered our hearts and we welcomed a new day.

10

Why me?

Again there began our long pedestrial trek as we neared the winters, it was really a bad news for us cause in winter the sun got tired too fast I guess and it soon gets dark and frosty.

Good thing I had planned for winters and packed up a few of dad's coats and jackets from his wardrobe.

-"Hold this" I threw the jacket at Joe "There it is, good thing that you think for."

-"You know I am cool" I said this in a weird accent and all the three of us got burst into laughter. Soon in realised that it was only about 60 kilometers left for for reaching the tower and

unfolding another mystery that awaited us. But those 60 kilometers would definitely not be easy.

Slowly the sunshine faded and we walked the fastest we could, we kept walking for 2-3 days skipping precious night sleeps and feeding or what ever we saw that seemed somewhat edible.

"Hey Vika, do you ever feel about our expressions if we achieve our mission successfully?" asked Joe. "I've gotta feel about that if we are alive that long" Jonathan said.

-"But all that was in my life now is that we accomplish our job, whatever that may cost us, it costed dad's and Liana's life but if it asks mine too I am always ready". I said wait a deep feeling the made my voice high with I don't know some sort of possesiveness towards people that still breathe.

They both nodded as we sat on huge rocks trying figure out the direction in which we had to move on. Sometimes I just thought that 'why me?' But the next moment I realised maybe 'why not me?'. And I must admit that Joe and Jonathan are really strong boys, they really formed a shield for me but I never let myself be their weakness I was strong enough on myself I guess but without them; difficulties would have hailed above me and I can't even imagine even taking a step towards something like this, something this unexpected.

I always imagined the future so as to have flying cars, tall buildings, robots, sensored cars, the tallest skyscrapers and what not maybe, but my life from beginning was unexpected, I never knew I'd lose mom at so early age after which dad became my world and then I suddenly lost dad and now the world became my life.

"I guess our madam is lost again"

Joe and Jonathan laughed but this time I was silent and realised their significance in my life will we talk about their stinky smelling bodies which even repelled mosquitoes from getting near them, but yeah who would not smell, not bathing for so long.

11

A shocking news

Suddenly and the most luckily my eyes caught hold of a standing sign board, it was actually quite difficult to notice it because it beautifully merged with the nature with the vines covering it, and there were 3 signs showing 3 different directions and way in which we were moving was 'Doxemberg - 50 miles'.

-"Yeah! That's where the 'D Tower' is" exclaimed Joe.

-"But it still says 50 miles, uff" I was penalised by a headache.

-"So what? You are tired by now only? We haven't yet reached there and after reaching the mystery is yet to be solved." said Mr. angry

Jonathan. As we were getting closed to our destination we found a lot obstacles from the metropolitan which clearly depicted a war that may have occured between the zombies and the men.

It was night, as the sapphire moonlight navigated our path and we slowly began to come across small societies of up to 5-6 people dwelling in utmost fear and anxiety. In one such society we stopped for one night stay where we came across and middle aged man of around 45, He claimed that he was a doctor back when everything was normal. And there we came to know another shocking fact.

12

Squad up!

"The Virus has mutated and the ones affected by this new strain creates mutants". He exclaimed.

-Can we know a bit more about this Doctor? - we enquired. He began speaking out all the knowledge he had-

"When a virus mutates it changes its form and creates a difference to the result that the unmutated virus led to, the unmutated virus created zombies but the new strain causes the infected a sudden increase in the height and structure of the body, they do look huge but they are only as powerful as the earlier ones but that is only because you are armoured with guns till now. So you guys better stop doing whatever you're doing and I believe it will all stop on its

own."

-"Who are you to stop us?"- Joe quirked.

Dr. Xuan, the inventer of the virus, it was not intentional, I just wanted to create a bit of time for the people," He replied. Jonathan grabbed his color and said

-"You! You began everything and you don't even aquire a sacred intention to cure it."

-Listen kid, I wanted to create an antidote as soon as I realised that the virus had leaked but the people captured me in a prison and destroyed my lab and burnt the formula papers of how I created this, otherwise I could definitely work on finding the cure but now there's no choice" Dr. Xuan sighed.

"You have such a huge head don't you even remember a thing?" interrogated Jonathan, but I always had a habit to laugh at serious situation and so did I which attracted everyone's weird eyes to me. "Guys no use fighting and will Jonathan beating him up find us a cure? Just calm down and Dr. Xuan would you like to be a part of us?

His eyes filled and he nodded a yes with a sense of respect. Next up we had a very small distance to cover and huge mystry to solve.

And voila! We were 4 again.

13

A small way and a huge secret

The journey ahead only consisted of walking and walking and... only walking. It was winter and therefore walking actually helped us stay warm but everytime we rested for a while the fear of not achieving what we were up to, held me tight and sometimes this extreme level of stress caused me anxiety attacks and I stared shivering and eventually collapsed.

But Joe and Jonathan, they always made sure I was comfortable, but after doctor Xuan joined us he told me some meditation and stuff which helped me to stay calm and not panic and that actually helped me a lot, reduced my panic attacks and things went on better.

The population of the world must have reached 11,000 and the scariest part remains the rest dead were not still, they moved, to quench their thirst they drank blood but luckily not all gets converted to zombies, some also face death otherwise it would have been impossible even to step out.

On our way we could see log stretches of land and huge pile of obviously; dead bodies but a thing that was shocking was that there were very few of the zombies we were now more like usual to them but the new varient; it was a mystery. It was the third night when we restarted our journey with Doc but one night, as we rested under a roof all asleep and I and Doc stayed awake to just keep a watch as I said we only slept on alternate days. Just then we both heard a sound from just outside the building we took shelter in, Dr. Xuan got up and said. "Calm down, let me just have a look, I will be back within 10 mins if not, I want you to just peep out and check if am alive and need help."

I nodded and he patted on my head and went outside as I stayed in the dark silence for his return. Waiting such around almost 9 minutes has past and I started worrying... he had not yet returned, I got quite scared and started poking Joe and Jonathan, but somehow I was able to pull Joe up out of his half- dead sleep, and I was about to step outside, looking for him just then he entered and slammed the door as he respired ponderously...

14

Confrontment, infection and change.

-"I-I-I saw that" -"saw what Dr.?" I queried. -"The new mutant of the virus, its huge and looks much more stronger". -"Did you kill it, or is it still alive?". -"I dont know, its dead or not all I know is I survived it" We all were undertaken with a fear, was the monster alive? What if it would jump on us as soon as we step outside. No one knew what was infront of us and empty path or an undefined death.

I was stuck between my feelings, just than Jonathan woke up and he interupted our conversation. -"I will go check out, if its dead or alive." I tried a lot to stop him but he never heard a word of mine. He wrapped a torn jacket around his arm (so that the zombie couldn't bit him easily) and walked outside as brave as fire.

He walked outside and soon I could hear a face slam.

I ran outside wondering if the reciever of the slam was Jonathan. When I peeped out of the door and saw Jonathan, he slammed the zombie with a huge plank of wood right on his face, no wonder it was huge it was tall and stout firmly built and now dead... After it died we took a sigh of relief as we decided to move on. After two more days as we decided to stop as Dr. Xuan started suffering from severe fever and headache as his eyes turned red, I made him lay down with a wet cloth in his head so, as to reduce fever but it had laready been 5-7 hours but nor did his fever decrease neither his eyes were back to normal. Rather his nerves started to grow wild as they popped out of his skin and he started coughing along with a sudden change in the behaviour.

The night darkened as we all went to sleep with him by my side, soon tiredness made me fast asleep lost in my dreams. I suddenly could hear groans, I didn't wake up until I felt a liquid drop on my cheek, I slightly opened my eyes just to see doctor dropping his saliva over me ready enought to devour my blood. I pushed him away with all my might and luckily enough he didn't bit my hand and weird enough that he didn't changed the way he looked he didn't yet looked like a zombie, but he behaved such, when I pushed him back and get away waking along Jonathan and Joe, he didn't get up, he laid down, still breathing, we three were creeped out because our life was in danger now, we thought of killing him when he was still unconcious, but he was the only hope who could make or find the cure, still our lives couldn't be risked so I went to him with an iron rod and as I lifted the rod to smash his face with it, "Stop" he said.

He sounded weak but he use all his might to speak up and then he began coughing, after some time, even in with immense fear, I went near to check his fever, his forehead was now cool, "he recovered?" I exclaimed "But how?" queried Jonathan, we didn't wake doctor so as to let him sleep and get better and we spent the night sitting next to him by a safe distance, early morning the sun came out and the early rays touched his eyes and he woke up. As fresh as a daisy, as if nothing had ever happened. "Are you alright?" I asked "surprisingly I am" he replied, "But I found something amazing" he added. "What ??" I, Jonathan and Joe asked together...

15

The cure?

"The cure will be much easier to find", he began "I remember when I was injecting the rat I didn't use anesthesia for it because it was tiny and I could control it, but when I pricked him in with the syringe his feet touched it and the needle pricked in through my silicon gloves, then maybe some particles of that vaccine had entered my body but as the dosage was less my body's immune system fought it and created an antibody, this means the cure is in my blood and the symbiote in the lab with whose plasma I made the vaccine. "That sounded like some Quantum physics" spoke Joe as crap as he always did "Shut up dude", "How far do you think your lab is from here?"

I asked doctor as I gave a dead stare to Jonathan, he laughed, "I don't know this place, but it musn't be that far, I was carried to that house by a jeep and have no idea of the distance by feet" said doctor, but we had to start again. Still we decided to spend one more night there and let doc be well and fine, I slept next to Jonathan, he was grown up into huge, tall, handsome, stout and strong guy, just like dad, I had slept behind him, I couldn't sleep, Jonathan turned to face me and I pretended to be asleep, and there came his huge hand wrapping half of my body into him, Oh! how warm that felt, how shy I was in there but how cozy it was and soon I felt asleep under his warm breaths. Morning I woke earlier than him but I still didn't move an inch beacuse I felt perfectly warm there, soon I felt he was about to wake up so I instantly closed my eyes and he woke up, finding me still asleep, he kissed me on the forehead and I blused, and to hide that I pretended to wake up just a few seconds after that, oh silly me, or was I falling for him? whatever it was, it felt beautiful, just as this was happening Joe pretended a cough,

-"You guys done? can we start over now?", asked Joe as we all laughed together, but you remember that symbiote? Was it still possible possible to find that thing in the lab or even the lab was destroyed, this was still a mystery, but one thing was final now the symbiote was the cure and to find it was our mission and the mission was to be completed so we started our expedition once again.

16

The end or the Beginning?

We walked till the late evening that day and as the sky darkened Jonathan said, "Hey look there the D Tower symbol" we all looked towards the side he pointed and Lo! he was not joking we could see the tiny red light at the top of the building and the huge building itself.

Now just a walk of 500 metres to reach there and unfold the mystery, cure and to which depended the earth's time ahead... We were all happy but couldn't shout so as not attract any more zombies, we all were actually filled with mixed emotions, very nervous, excited and terrified at the some time, we literally started running till there. And finally we were here, the building with 15 floors stood with firmness, the ground floor was completely destroyed but as we headed towards the higher floor there were huge iron doors with special scanning and voice recognization system then we finally reached the 7th floor and there Dr.Xuan placed his hand on the scanner screen. "Welcome Dr.Xuan Verendez" said a robotic voice from around the room which echoed in the visual silence, we all entered and were sprayed with probably sanitizing liquid.

As we entered inside I noticed a glass box which contained a jelly like structure, black in colour, that was the symbiote! The boys were looking out of the glass walls, everything so different from that height.

*I walked near the symbiote to have a closer look. I couldn't resist myself from touching the box and so did I, just then a squeak and a mouse hopped on me and dig his tiny teeth deep in my hand, Joe noticing that tried shooting at the tiny mouse cause he knew this was just '**The Mouse**', his first shot killed the mouse and created a hole in the glass box, but in vain, I was already bitten, all my hope ended I sat down on the floor, doctor who went looking for his research papers came running to me, Jonathan with his soul halfway out held doctor's color and I could hear him. "Go and find the cure, save her".*

"I need some time" he said as my vision blurred. Suddenly the symbiote squeezed out the tiny

bullet hole, it wrapped my hand, I could still feel it and the I opened my eyes!

"I-I am fine? How?" Jonathan came running and hugged me, for he really cared. "I was cured by the symbiote", I shouted "We found the cure, doctor" he was quite surprised, and as genuinely he pulled out the symbiote of my hand and said "follow me!" We entered the lift and the door opened at the terrace, there was a huge, tall machine. "Air infuser?" I read "Yes", said doctor "As the name suggests it can vapourize everything so that it gets mixed in the air, so he pulled out the capsule present inside, refilled it with the symbiote and put the capsule back to the machine.

"Initiating in 10... 9" the machine started, we stood together and held hands firm, we were filled with happiness and immense satisfaction... Just then I saw a zombie in the street below, from above the 15 floors, it just seemed like a tiny moving dot. Joe was about to shoot it and,

"Stop!" I said "Don't shoot we will see the effect on it". So he put back his gun. "3...2...1 launching" and all the vapour sprayed into the air got all of us a little sneeze, we all looked at the zombie below, it had stopped banging its

own head on the tree, soon he fainted as he seemed severly hurt by what he did to himself. "I think it is safe to go and spectate it" said Doc. So we all went downstairs and rushed to that zombie, it had gravely hurt itself banging the head on the tree, we took some water and sprinkled in his face, he opened his eyes. We all looked at each other crying with joy, he too seemed to be having a blurred vision but as soon as he was in his senses, he sat up and vomited just there, maybe for the blood he had already devoured on!

Just then an alarmic sound began to ring continuously, I looked around but no one else did. I was the only one who could hear that? I opened my eyes and What? I was in my room...and my body began feeling like a rusted machine that laid in the corner since long, and as I unfolded the curtains of my window, I saw a man walking aimlessly dragging his blooded feet, was he hurt..as i was initiating that in my mind he soon jumped over the lady walking past and now it had all really began..

I walked to dad soon as soon as I saw that, and ever as I dreamt he was surprised to see me and, got old in one night? Or just my dream turned into a vision..?

9 798886 847895

Printed by Libri Plureos GmbH in Hamburg, Germany